22182896

SUNNYSIDE
PRIMARY SCHOOL

Alice Knows Best

Written by **Karen Wallace**
Illustrated by Bob Dewar

A & C Black • London

For Harvey James Gray

First published 2008 by
A & C Black Publishers Ltd
38 Soho Square, London, W1D 3HB

www.acblack.com

Text copyright © 2008 Karen Wallace
Illustrations copyright © 2008 Bob Dewar

The rights of Karen Wallace and Bob Dewar to be identified as the
author and illustrator of this work respectively has been asserted by them
in accordance with the Copyrights, Designs and Patents Act 1988.

ISBN 978-0-7136-8816-0

A CIP catalogue for this book is available from the British Library.

Printed and bound in Singapore by Tien Wah Press (Pte) Ltd

Chapter One

Alice was an anteater who lived in the jungle. Every day, she dug for ants with her sharp, curved claws and slurped them up with her long tongue.

One day, while the other anteaters were snoozing in the sunshine, Alice went down to the river to visit Cornelius the Crocodile. Cornelius loved talking and always told great stories.

At first, Alice couldn't find him. Then she heard a noise like a crocodile crying. She peered through the reeds and saw Cornelius lying in the water. Big, fat tears were pouring down his nose.

"*Boo, hoo*!" sobbed Cornelius. "I'm *so* lonely! Everyone has a friend except me!"

"Don't be sad, Cornelius," said Alice, climbing onto a rock. Alice liked Cornelius, but sometimes he forgot his manners and gobbled up his visitors by mistake. "I'm your friend. The other anteaters are your friends, too."
"But I want a friend to *play* with," cried Cornelius. "There's no one in the river but me."

Alice frowned. The last time she had visited Cornelius, he had been talking to a huge fish with long whiskers. "What happened to that catfish?" she asked. "It swam away," muttered Cornelius.

Alice didn't have to ask why. Even so, she still felt sorry for Cornelius. He had helped her in the past. Now it was her turn to help him.

"OK," said Alice. "I promise to find you a friend, but you have to promise *me* something, too."
"*Anything*!" cried Cornelius.

"No one will be your friend if you're always trying to eat them," said Alice, firmly. "You must keep your mouth shut!"

"I'll try," replied Cornelius. Then he sank into the river, looking sadder than ever.

Chapter Two

The next day, Alice asked all the other anteaters to come to her place. She told them about Cornelius and how lonely he was, but none of them knew what to do.

"I know," said one anteater at last. "Let's dig up a few ants and have a snooze in the sunshine."
Then they all ran off before Alice had time to reply.

"Why don't you look in your magazines,"
said Alice's mother, who was busy making
ant jam. "They might give you an idea."

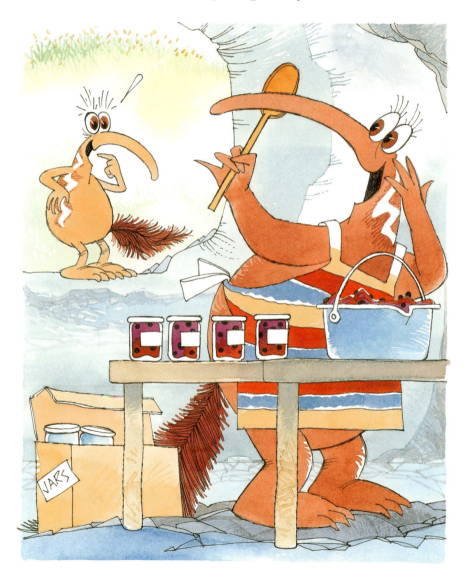

So Alice went to the hollow tree trunk where she kept her magazines. Cornelius had found them in the river and she had dried them out in the sun.

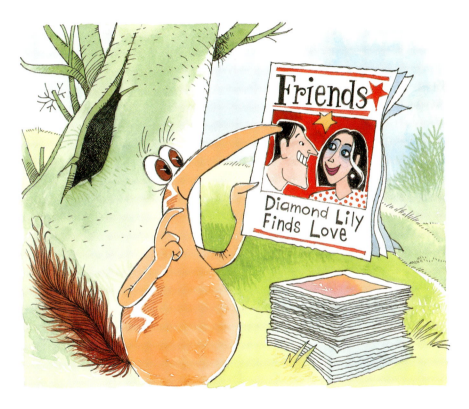

At the top of the pile was one called *Friends* with a picture of two movie stars smiling at each other. "Diamond Lily Finds Love" was written underneath.

Alice turned over the page and read
how the movie star had put up a notice
on the door of her dressing room.
"WANTED! Someone as wonderful
as me!" it had said.

A grin spread across Alice's face. She took out a piece of paper and wrote:

Then she drew lots of pictures around the edge to make the paper look pretty, and pinned it to a tree.

Two days later, the only reply Alice had received was from a parrot that talked so much, she nearly drove Cornelius crazy.

In the end, the crocodile shut his great jaws together with such a loud *SNAP* that the parrot flew off, squawking at the top of her voice.

"Really, Cornelius," said Alice crossly. "Don't you think that was rather rude?" "Not as rude as that parrot," replied Cornelius. "She wouldn't let me get a word in edgeways." He ran his pink tongue over his teeth. "I should have—"

But Alice was already on her way back to the jungle. It was clear that everyone here knew too much about Cornelius. If she was going to find him a friend, she would have to look further away.

Chapter Three

"Are you sure that's a good idea?"
asked Alice's mother, when she heard
Alice was going off on a trip.

"I know best, Mother," said Alice, firmly.
"I promised to help Cornelius and I
always keep my promises."
"Of course, dear," replied Alice's mother
as she stuck labels onto pots of ant jam.
"When will you be back?"

"In two days," said Alice. "In time for tea!" She was looking forward to eating the ant jam. Then she kissed her mother goodbye, picked up her favourite pink handbag and set off towards the river.

Cornelius poked his head above the water as Alice climbed onto her raft.

"Why do you have to go down the river?" asked Cornelius.

"Because everyone around here knows you," replied Alice.

Cornelius made a huffing sound. "What's that supposed to mean?"

"I think you know the answer to that," said Alice. "By the way, do you mind if I look in your dressing up box?"
"Help yourself," said Cornelius in a sulky voice. "You know where it is." Then he swam off before Alice could say goodbye.

At first, Alice couldn't make up her mind what to wear. A pretty, frilly dress?

Or a plain trouser suit with black buttons?

At last, she picked a turquoise jacket with padded shoulders to make her look bigger, and a matching skirt with a slit up the side in case she had to run fast. Then, as a finishing touch, she chose a pair of fancy shoes with spiky heels and a hat with a ribbon.

Now she was ready for *anything*!

Chapter Four

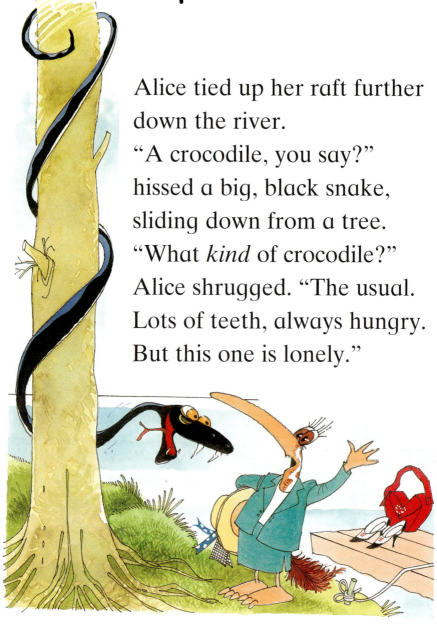

Alice tied up her raft further
down the river.
"A crocodile, you say?"
hissed a big, black snake,
sliding down from a tree.
"What *kind* of crocodile?"
Alice shrugged. "The usual.
Lots of teeth, always hungry.
But this one is lonely."

"A *lonely* crocodile, you say," hissed
the snake, moving closer. "So he wants
a friend, perhaps."

"Exactly," replied Alice, picking up her
pink handbag and putting on her shoes.
"That's why I'm here. I promised to
help him."

"I *like* an anteater who keeps a promise,"
hissed the snake, almost in Alice's ear.

There was something in the snake's voice.
Or maybe it was the way he said the word
"like"… Alice spun round. She was
looking upwards into the snake's mouth!
Quick as flash, she bashed him on the
head with her handbag.

But it didn't make any difference!

"I *love* an anteater with a temper,"
hissed the snake, as he slid onto the
ground and wrapped himself around
Alice's legs.
Now Alice was looking *down* into the
snake's mouth and his fangs were
coming closer! *Two* fangs!

Alice's heart thumped hard. She grabbed her hat and stuffed it down the snake's mouth.

Then before he had time to spit it out, she whipped off her shoes and bashed them on either side of his head!

As the snake fell back, Alice hit him with her paddle and sent him flying through the air. He landed on the other side of the river with a *thump*.

Alice squared her shoulders and straightened her skirt. It was dangerous work finding a friend for a crocodile.

Chapter Five

For the next two days, Alice spoke to every animal she met. But most of them had friends of their own and weren't interested in meeting a crocodile.

"I wouldn't mind," said a monkey with a sly look on his face. "I could run up and down his tail until he got really cross." "That doesn't sound very nice," said Alice. The monkey shrugged. "I'm not." Then he dropped a mango on Alice's head and ran off howling with laughter.

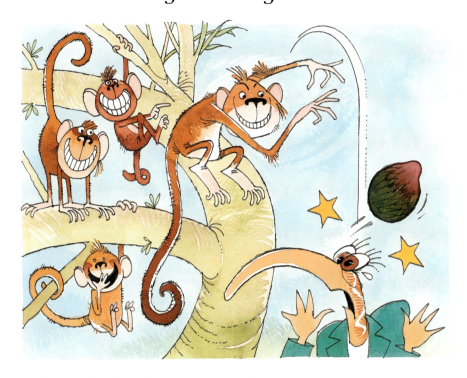

Alice sighed. The monkey was even more badly behaved than Cornelius.

Further up the shore, an odd animal with a long snout was paddling in the river. "What are you?" asked Alice.
"I'm a sort of rhinoceros, but I look like a pig," it shrugged. "I'm called a tapir."

Alice had never heard of a tapir before, but she knew Cornelius liked swimming. "Would you like to be a friend to a crocodile?" she asked.
"As long as he's not called Cornelius," said the tapir.

Alice was so surprised, she sat down on a rock. "You know him!" she gasped. "He tried to bite me when I was little," replied the tapir, climbing out of the water. "When I asked him not to, he laughed and said it would toughen me up."

"Of course, now I have very thick skin on my back," said the tapir, rolling in the mud. "But I would never trust Cornelius again. If he wants a friend, he will have to change his ways."

Alice got up from her rock. "Thank you," she said. "You are right. And I'm going back to tell him so."

Chapter Six

Alice was just about to set off, when
she heard a noise like a crocodile crying.
"*Boo*, *hoo*," sobbed the voice. "I wish
I had a friend. I'm *so* lonely."

Alice could hardly believe her ears. She paddled along the bank to get nearer. In the middle of the reeds was a crocodile with tears pouring down its nose.

"Excuse me," said Alice, kindly. Although she didn't want to get too close because it was a crocodile, after all. "My name is Alice and I might be able to help you." The crocodile looked up. "My name is Cornelia," she said. Another tear rolled down her nose. "But no one around here likes me and it's all my fault."

Alice moved a little further away. "Why is it all your fault?" she asked, though she was pretty sure she knew the answer. Cornelia looked down at the water. "It's my manners," she said sadly. "The problem is that sometimes I forget them and—"

"You don't have to explain," interrupted Alice. "Follow me! I think I know just the friend for you!" And she picked up her paddle and headed home.

Chapter Seven

There were lots of brown tails waggling in the grass as Alice floated towards the shore. News travels fast in the jungle and she knew the other anteaters couldn't wait to find out what would happen when the two crocodiles met.

Alice pointed to where Cornelius was lying in the water. "He's over there," she said to Cornelia. "Go and tell him you want to be his friend."

"But what if he doesn't like me?" wailed Cornelia.

"Trust me," said Alice. "I know best."

She watched as Cornelia swam in a circle around Cornelius. When she stopped, Cornelius swam in a circle around her.

Suddenly Cornelius leapt out of the water and twirled in the air. Cornelia leapt up beside him! They were friends at first sight!

The next minute, Cornelius zoomed up beside Alice's raft and hung his great head at her feet. There were tears in his eyes. "You're a good friend, Alice," he sobbed. "You've made me very, very happy."

"That's all right, Cornelius," said Alice. "I always keep my promises. Now go off to play with Cornelia and you'll never be lonely again."

Alice stepped onto the shore and pulled off her suit. It was tea time and she was hungry. Then her mother appeared carrying a cake. "Surprise!" she cried.

All the anteaters laughed and Alice gave her mother a big hug. Across the top of the cake, written in big, white letters, were the words ALICE KNOWS BEST!

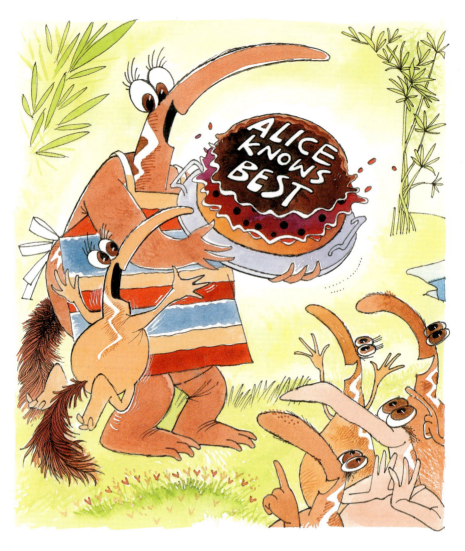